WILL'S MAMMOTH

STORY BY RAFE MARTIN

ILLUSTRATED BY STEPHEN GAMMELL

G.P. PUTNAM'S SONS

To a certain BOULDER of my childhood, which TAUGHT me that STONES can live. And to MINNIE WOLF... she DREAMED DREAMS and SAW VISIONS.

Dave

To GRETCHEN, SARAH and BEN.

Stephen

WILL LOVED MAMMOTHS...

...WOOLLY
MAMMOTHS.

HIS MOTHER and FATHER HAD TOLD HIM THAT ALL THE MAMMOTHS HAD DISAPPEARED TEN THOUSAND YEARS AGO.

"THERE AREN'T ANY MORE MAMMOTHS, WILL— ANYWHERE."

BUT WILL KNEW THAT THERE WERE.

"WiLL, iT'S GETTiNG DARK! TiME FOR SUPPER!"

"WHAT DID
YOU DO
TODAY,
WILL?"

"I
RODE
MY
MAMMOTH."

"GOOD NIGHT," Will whispered. "I'LL SEE YOU TOMORROW."

EDUCATION LIBRARY
UNIVERSITY OF KENTUCKY